Team Stats—Football Edition

HIGHLIGHTS OF THE INDIANAPOLIS COLTS

MARYSA STORM

BLACK RABBIT BOOKS

Bolt is published by Black Rabbit Books
P.O. Box 277, Mankato, Minnesota, 56002.
www.blackrabbitbooks.com

Jennifer Besel, editor; Michael Sellner, interior designer; Grant Gould, cover designer; Omay Ayres, photo researcher

Library of Congress Cataloging-in-Publication Data
Names: Storm, Marysa, author.
Title: Highlights of the Indianapolis Colts / by Marysa Storm.
Description: Mankato, Minnesota : Black Rabbit Books, [2020] | Series: Bolt. Team stats—football edition | Includes bibliographical references and index.
Identifiers: LCCN 2018053519 (print) | LCCN 2018059245 (ebook) | ISBN 9781680728927 (ebook) | ISBN 9781680728866 (library binding) | ISBN 9781644660836 (paperback)
Subjects: LCSH: Indianapolis Colts (Football team)—Juvenile literature.
Classification: LCC GV956.I53 (ebook) | LCC GV956.I53 S86 2020 (print) | DDC 796.332/640977252—dc23
LC record available at https://lccn.loc.gov/2018053519

Printed in the United States of America.

Image Credits

AP Images: Aaron M. Sprecher, Cover; AP, 11; AP, 20 (t); Jack Dempsey, 21; LIEBB, 22 (l); Ryan Kang, 28–29 (t); commons.wikimedia.org: 13; Baltimore Sun, 6 (b); Mr.schultz, 6 (t); Getty: Andy Lyons, 3, 16–17 (bkgd); Bettmann, 24–25; Donald Miralle, 8; Doug Benc, 14–15; Focus on Sport, 12; Gregory Shamus, 22–23 (Harrison); Jim McIsaac, 23 (r); Tom Dahlin, 16–17 (Luck); Tom Hauck, 4–5; TOM MIHALEK, 26; Tony Tomsic, 18–19; Newscom: BRENT SMITH/REUTERS, 20 (b); John Mersits/Cal Sport Media, 1; Shutterstock: EFKS, 22–23 (bkgd); enterlinedesign, 28–29 (b); Svyatoslav Aleksandrov, 31; VitaminCo, 10, 19, 32

Every effort has been made to contact copyright holders for material reproduced in this book. Any omissions will be rectified in subsequent printings if notice is given to the publisher.

CONTENTS

Touchdown!

CHAPTER 1

On the FIELD

The Indianapolis Colts had taken the lead in a 2005 game. Quarterback Peyton Manning prepared to make another pass. The ball soared through the air and into Marvin Harrison's hands. Touchdown! But it wasn't just any touchdown pass. It was Manning's 86th touchdown pass to Harrison. The Colts didn't just win the game. They set a new record.

CHAPTER 2

HISTORY of the Colts

The Colts is a powerful team. But it had a rocky beginning. In 1946, the Miami Seahawks moved to Baltimore. It became the Colts. Unfortunately, the **franchise** didn't make enough money. It **dissolved** in 1951. The Dallas Texans moved to Baltimore in 1953. It became the new Colts. Then in 1984, the team moved to Indianapolis.

The owner moved the team to Indianapolis in secret. A new law said Baltimore could take the team from him. He moved out before the city could act.

SUPER BOWL
ONE DREAM
SUPER BOWL XLI

Winning Big

No matter the city, the new Colts won big games. The team won championship games in 1958, 1959, and 1968. It won the Super Bowl in 1971. After several slow seasons, the team improved in the early 2000s. In 2007, Manning led it to win another Super Bowl.

CHAPTER 3

Greatest MOMENTS

The Colts has played many amazing games. The team played the New York Giants in the 1958 Championship. They battled the entire game. A last-minute touchdown by the Colts tied the game. It went into overtime. The Colts then made a game-winning touchdown.

This game was the first game to be nationally televised. It was also the first championship to go into overtime. People call it "The Greatest Game Ever Played."

1969 Super Bowl vs. New York Jets
LOSS 7-16

1971 Super Bowl vs. Dallas Cowboys
WIN 16-13

2007 Super Bowl vs. Chicago Bears
WIN 29-17

2010 Super Bowl vs. New Orleans Saints
LOSS 17-31

Colts' Super Bowl Scores

1971 Super Bowl

In 1971, the Colts won its first Super Bowl. At first, it didn't look like it'd win. The Dallas Cowboys led most of the game. But in the fourth quarter, the Colts tied it up. Then with only seconds left, kicker Jim O'Brien made a field goal.

2007 Super Bowl

The Colts played its third Super Bowl in 2007. Right away, things looked bad. The Bears soared to an early lead. It was raining too. But the Colts wouldn't let the Bears or the weather stop them.

In the second quarter, the Colts picked up speed. The team soon took the lead. In the fourth quarter, a Colts player **intercepted** the ball. He took it in for a touchdown.

BY THE NUMBERS

(as of 2018)

most receptions in a single season
(Colts player Marvin Harrison)

143

total retired jersey numbers

7

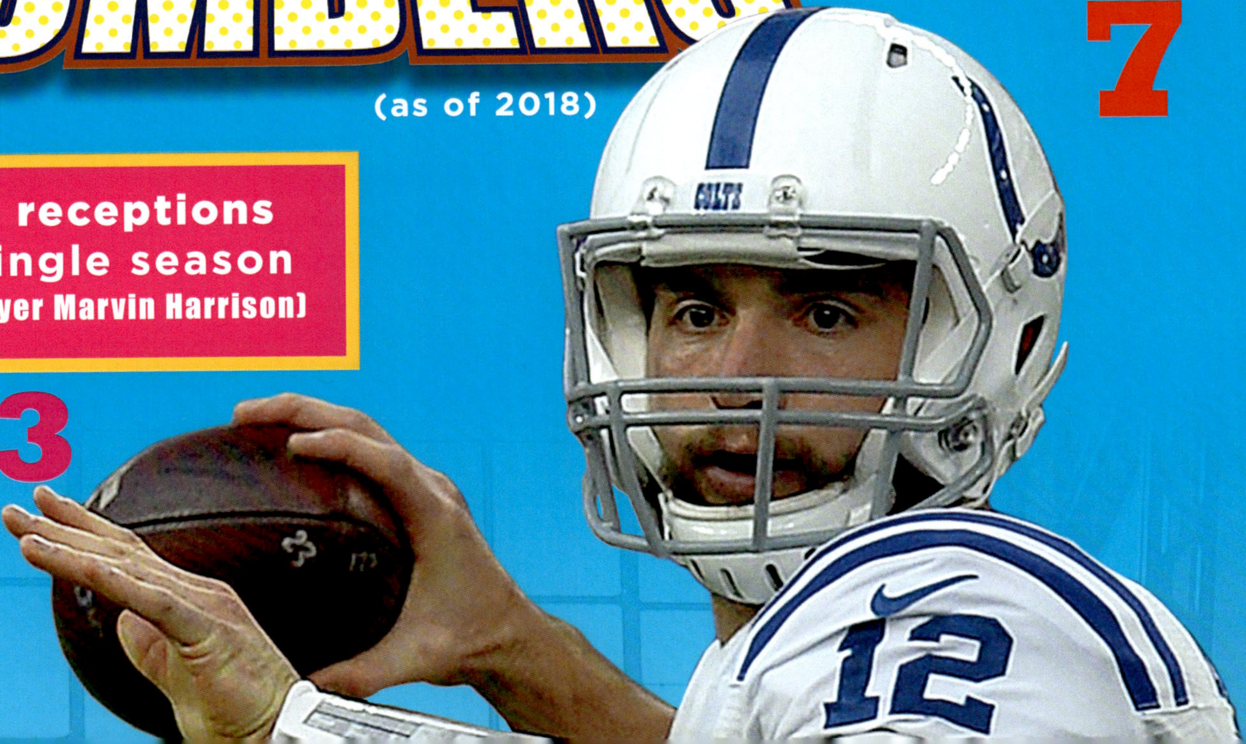

4,761 yards

team record for most passing yards in one season (Andrew Luck)

112 touchdowns

most touchdowns made between one quarterback and receiver
(Colts players Peyton Manning and Marvin Harrison)

44

most field goals made in a row
(Colts player Adam Vinatieri)

CHAPTER 4

STARS of the Colts

Many football stars have played as Colts. One of the greatest was Johnny Unitas. Unitas was an incredible quarterback. He set 22 records during 17 seasons with the Colts.

Unitas' NFL Records at Retirement

most passes attempted
5,186

most passes completed
2,830

most yards gained
40,239

most touchdown passes
290

Top Colts Receivers

Raymond Berry

Marvin Harrison

Reggie Wayne

Receivers

The Colts has had many amazing receivers. From 1955 to 1967, Raymond Berry played for the Colts. Many people consider him the **era's** best receiver. He retired as the all-time reception leader.

Marvin Harrison also ranks at the top. He made incredible catches.

Another great receiver was Reggie Wayne. Wayne played more games than any other Colt. He now helps coach Colts' wide receivers.

Comparing Colts' Top Receivers

	Raymond Berry
total games played	154
career catches	631
career receiving yards	9,275
most touchdowns in a single season	14
career touchdowns	68

Marvin Harrison	Reggie Wayne
190	211
1,102	1,070
14,580	14,345
15	12
128	82

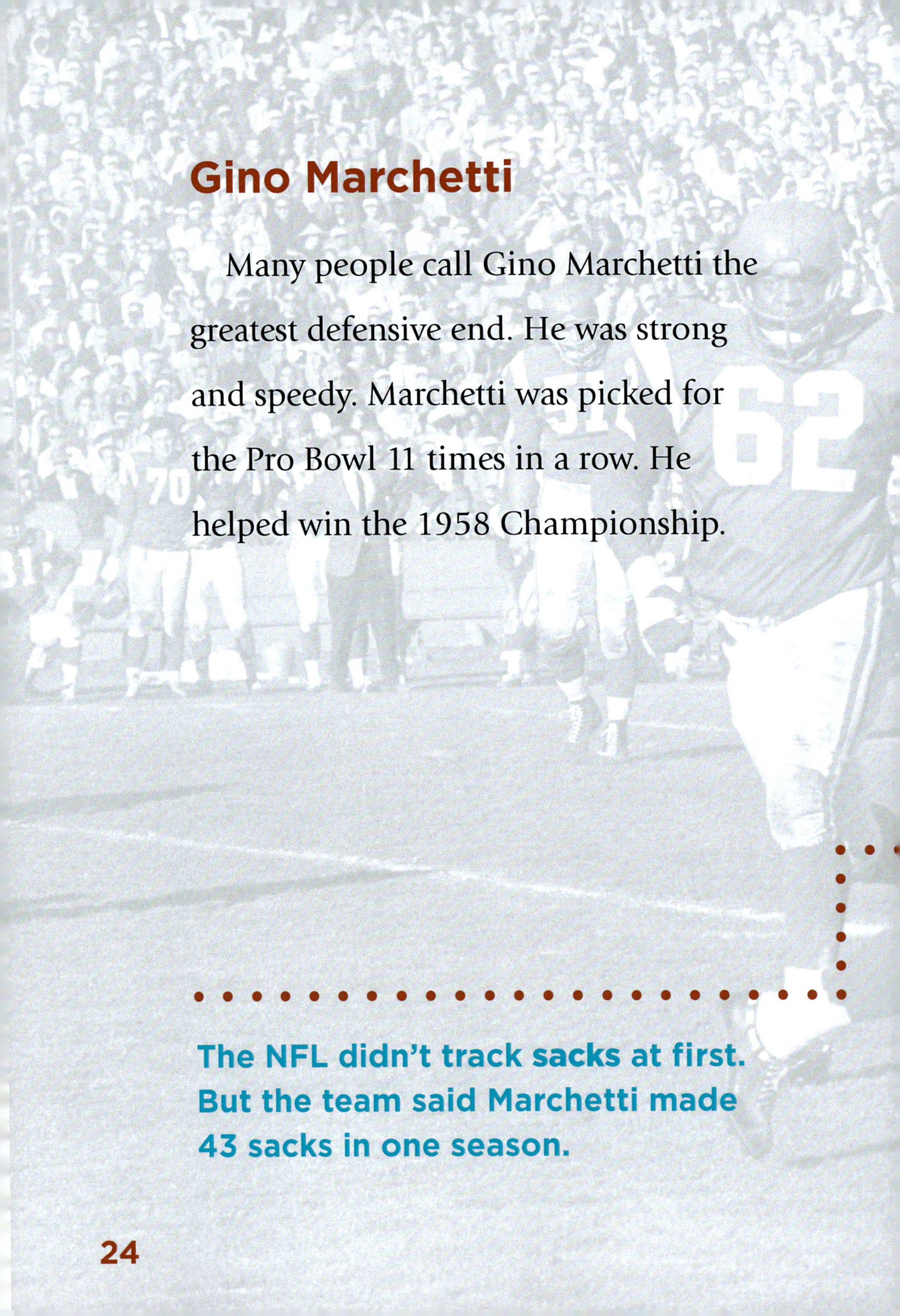

Gino Marchetti

Many people call Gino Marchetti the greatest defensive end. He was strong and speedy. Marchetti was picked for the Pro Bowl 11 times in a row. He helped win the 1958 Championship.

The NFL didn't track sacks at first. But the team said Marchetti made 43 sacks in one season.

Manning has a record five AP MVP Awards.

Peyton Manning

Unitas wasn't the Colts' only powerful quarterback. In 1998, the Colts **drafted** Peyton Manning. He quickly became one of the NFL's top quarterbacks. As of 2018, he holds the record for most career touchdown passes.

From a tough start to big wins, fans have stuck with the Colts. They can't wait to see what the team does next.

TIMELINE

1950

1953
First season as new Colts.

1956
Unitas joins Colts.

1958
Team wins "The Greatest Game Ever Played."

1971
Colts win its first Super Bowl.

1984
Team moves to Indianapolis.

1998
Colts draft Manning.

2007
Team wins its second Super Bowl.

2016
Harrison enters Pro Football Hall of Fame.

2020

GLOSSARY

career (kuh-REER)—a period of time spent in a job

dissolve (di-ZOLV)—to bring to an end

draft (DRAFT)—to pick a player for a professional team through a specialized system

era (AYR-uh)—a period of time identified by a major event, person, or stage of development

franchise (FRAN-chiz)—a team and its operating organization

intercept (in-tur-SEPT)—to catch a pass made by the other team

receiver (reh-SEE-vur)—a football player who catches passes thrown by the quarterback

reception (ree-SEP-shun)—catching a pass thrown toward an opponent's goal

retire (ree-TIYR)—to withdraw from use; it also means to stop playing a game or competition.

sack (SAK)—a tackle of the quarterback before he or she crosses the line of scrimmage

LEARN MORE

BOOKS

Burgess, Zack. *Meet the Indianapolis Colts.* Big Picture Sports. Chicago: Norwood House Press, 2017.

Murray, Laura K. *Andrew Luck.* The Big Time. Mankato, MN: Creative Education, 2017.

Osborne, M.K. *Superstars of the Indianapolis Colts.* Pro Sports Superstars NFL. Mankato, MN: Amicus, 2019.

WEBSITES

Football: National Football League
www.ducksters.com/sports/national_football_league.php

Indianapolis Colts Team Page
www.nfl.com/teams/indianapoliscolts/profile?team=ind

The Official Website of the Indianapolis Colts
www.colts.com

INDEX